This edition published by Parragon Books Ltd in 2016

Parragon Books Ltd
Chartist House
15–17 Trim Street
Bath BA1 1HA, UK
www.parragon.com

All stories based on the Marvel comic book series *The Avengers*.

Hulk SMASH! adapted by Clarissa Wong. Illustrated Ron Lim and Rachelle Rosenberg.
Black Widow Bites Back! adapted by Elizabeth Schaefer. Illustrated by Neil Edwards and Rachelle Rosenberg.
Falcon Earns His Wings written by Scott Peterson. Illustrated by Andrea Di Vito and Rachelle Rosenberg.
What Goes Up Must Come Down written by Ivan Cohen. Illustrated by Agustin Padilla and Rachelle Rosenberg.
Party Crashers written by Michael Siglain. Illustrated by Neil Edwards and Rachelle Rosenberg.
Battle for Earth! written by Patrick Olliffe. Illustrated by Khoi Pham and Paul Mounts.
Kang – Conqueror of S.H.I.E.L.D.! written by Bryan Q. Miller. Illustrated by Neil Edwards and Rachelle Rosenberg.
Call for Backup written by Chris "Doc" Wyatt. Illustrated by Khoi Pham and Paul Mounts.
An Unexpected Hero written by Chris "Doc" Wyatt. Illustrated by Neil Edwards and Rachelle Rosenberg.

ISBN 978-1-4748-3664-7

Printed in China

Storybook
Collection

Bath • New York • Cologne • Melbourne • Delhi
Hong Kong • Shenzhen • Singapore

Contents

Hulk SMASH!

Hulk is one of Earth's Mightiest Heroes. No one could deny his incredible strength or size. Whether fighting alone or side by side with the Avengers, he can take down almost any villain. Even villains as huge as he is are no problem! But before he became the incredible Hulk, he was just an ordinary man named Bruce Banner.

Bruce was a brilliant scientist. He used to spend his time studying a special kind of energy called gamma radiation. Bruce knew that gamma rays were dangerous, but he wanted to show the world they had good uses too!

Bruce decided that the best way to test the gamma rays' power was to set up an explosion. Then he could measure the radiation they gave off using special equipment.

Bruce carefully set up a testing site in the middle of the desert. He knew he needed to do his test in an empty place so no one would get hurt. But something terrible happened! A young boy wandered into the testing area.

Jumping into his car, Bruce raced off to save the boy.

Bruce arrived at the test site with only moments to spare! He grabbed the boy and threw him into a nearby bomb shelter. But Bruce was not so lucky. Before he could get himself to safety, his device exploded!

Bruce woke up in an army hospital. The army had found him in the desert and they were worried about him.

Bruce looked at himself in the mirror. He didn't feel sick, but he did feel ... different.

Suddenly, Bruce felt something strange. His head hurt and he let out a loud cry. Bruce looked down in shock. His skin was starting to turn green! Then his hands expanded and his muscles grew until he was four times his normal size.

Bruce knew the radiation from the blast was to blame, but he was powerless to stop the change that had come over him. In a fit of anger, Bruce smashed through the brick wall of the hospital and escaped. Some nearby soldiers saw him and yelled into their radios, "Look out for a green monster, a Goliath, a HULK!"

All Hulk wanted was to be left alone. He did not want to hurt anyone. But the army could not let the mysterious monster escape. A tank full of soldiers chased after him! The soldiers surrounded Hulk.

As the tank fired at Hulk, a rush of rage came over the green beast. He clenched his fists and roared, "HULK SMASH!"

Hulk easily lifted the large tank and threw it across the field. Then, before the fighting could start again, he leaped away. He did not want to fight.

Hulk ran until the soldiers were out of sight. When he was safely away, he tried to calm down.

As his anger eased, he felt his body change again. He became smaller and the green left his skin. Soon he was Bruce Banner once more.

Bruce wanted to keep the truth about Hulk a secret. He hoped he would never become Hulk again. But Hulk was not gone. Every time Bruce felt angry or frustrated, he transformed into Hulk.

Bruce tried to remain calm at all times, but when he saw Super Villains hurting innocent people, he could not stay calm. He wanted to defend the helpless. So did Hulk!

The problem was, people were scared of Hulk. They pointed and called him a monster.

This made Hulk sad. He thought that if he kept helping people, maybe they would realize he was friendly. But no matter how hard he tried, people still ran from him.

Slowly, Bruce realized that people who judged Hulk on his appearance were wrong!

Hulk knew that he could do great things for others. He could fight for those in trouble and save people from danger. The green Goliath was very powerful, and he wanted to use that power for good!

No matter how big or small the problem, Hulk was there to save the day. Hulk was a big hero with a big heart. The more good he did, the more people came to love him.

But there are times when a threat is too big for any one hero to handle, and so Hulk became part of the mighty team of Avengers. Now he stands proud among Captain America, Iron Man, Thor, Falcon, Black Widow and Hawkeye. Together, Hulk and the Avengers fight for the good of the world – just like Bruce Banner always wanted to do!

Black Widow Bites Back

Natasha Romanoff and her brother, Alexi, were orphans. The two had been raised at an orphanage known as the Red Room.

But the Red Room was really home to a secret Russian spy programme.

So Natasha and Alexi became spies. Together they went on missions to gather information about S.H.I.E.L.D. The two had just failed their most recent assignment. Now they were waiting outside the office of the Red Room's leader, Ivan Bezukhov.

"This is all my fault," Alexi said. "Every time we've failed, it's been because of something I messed up."

"Don't worry," Natasha replied. "I'll take care of you." But Natasha *was* worried. They had made too many mistakes lately, and Ivan was not a patient man.

"You're so good at this spy stuff, Natasha," Alexi told his sister. "You're like a black widow. I'm like a clumsy hippo, ruining everything."

"Natasha." Ivan's voice came from behind them. "I'll see you in my office now. Alone."

Natasha gave Alexi a reassuring smile, then stepped into Ivan's office.

"Today was not a good day for you, the Red Room, or – most importantly – me," Ivan said coldly. "Alexi has been the cause of too many failed missions. He must be disposed of."

"No!" Natasha cried.

Natasha knew that the Red Room disposed of failed spies by wiping their memories.

"If you erase his memory, he won't remember who *I* am," Natasha said. She knew she couldn't allow that to happen.

So she ran from Ivan's office, but she was too late. Red Room agents were already dragging her brother away.

Natasha fought her way to freedom. She would find a way to rescue Alexi, she had to....

Natasha went to the only people she knew who could help – her old enemy, S.H.I.E.L.D. Using her spy gear from the Red Room, Natasha reprogrammed an old S.H.I.E.L.D. identification badge to fool the security guards. Then, disguised as a cleaner, she sneaked into S.H.I.E.L.D. headquarters.

Natasha casually walked past the guard. Once he was out of sight, she slipped into an air vent.

A few twists and turns later, Natasha was directly above Director Nick Fury's office. Natasha flipped down on to Fury's desk. He was shocked! Before Fury could call security, Natasha asked him for his help – and his forgiveness.

"I know I've caused a lot of trouble for your team," Natasha told Fury, "but I'll do anything S.H.I.E.L.D. asks if you help me rescue my brother."

Fury reluctantly agreed. Natasha and Alexi *had* caused a lot of trouble, but he couldn't leave Alexi to the mercy of the Red Room.

Fury introduced Natasha to the Avengers. Natasha was surprised at how willing they were to help, even though none of them knew her.

"We'll rescue your brother," Captain America promised.

"Taking on the Red Room will be tricky, even for a super spy like you, Natasha," Tony Stark added. "I think you need some upgraded tech!"

That evening, Natasha led the Avengers to the Red Room's secret base. The Avengers freed Ivan's prisoners as they searched for Alexi.

Suddenly, Natasha heard a familiar voice behind her say, "I see you've come home." It was Ivan! The leader of the Red Room threw a punch at Natasha.

"Where is my brother?" Natasha asked, fighting Ivan off.

Ivan laughed as he blocked her every move.

"You can't hurt me," Ivan said.

"*I* can't, but I bet *this* will." Natasha fired a powerful electric blast from her gauntlet, knocking Ivan to the ground.

"What was that?" Ivan cried.

"An upgrade from Tony Stark. Now, where is my brother?"

Ivan knew he couldn't fight against the Avengers' technology. He told Natasha where to find Alexi.

Natasha rushed to Alexi's cell. His eyes were closed and he looked weak.

"Alexi," she called.

Alexi's eyes fluttered. "What – what are you doing here? I thought Ivan got rid of you…" he said.

"You're okay!" Natasha shouted, hugging her brother.

Natasha smiled up at the Avengers. She knew she couldn't have saved Alexi without them.

Later, back at S.H.I.E.L.D. headquarters, Nick Fury took Natasha aside. "I don't know many spies who would have been able to break into my office. Or who would risk their lives for someone else," he said. "I would like you to join Earth's mightiest team of Super Heroes, the Avengers. What do you say, Natasha?"

"Count me in!" Natasha said with a smile. "You can call me Black Widow."

Falcon Earns His Wings

Falcon.

An invaluable member of the Avengers.
One of Captain America's best friends.
A brave hero who has saved the lives of Iron Man, Thor and Hulk.
But he hasn't always been this way.

Once upon a time, Falcon was just a boy named Sam Wilson.

Young Sam grew up in a tough part of New York City. His parents did their best to love him, protect him and teach him right from wrong.

Sam had always felt a close connection with birds. His parents encouraged his love of animals. They even let him keep a pigeon coop on the roof of their apartment building.

But Sam lost his parents at an early age. Feeling hurt, scared and helpless, Sam decided the only way to survive was to become tougher and harder than anyone else.

Soon that was exactly what Sam was – tough! He did what it took to get ahead. But he always made sure to do what was right and stand up for others who felt as helpless as he once had.

To get a break from the city, Sam took a job on a strange island called the Isle of Exiles. But when he arrived, Sam discovered the island had been taken over by the evil Red Skull and his Hydra army!

Red Skull imprisoned Sam. He wanted him to work for Hydra. Sam managed to get away, but not before Red Skull gave him the ability to communicate with birds.

Sam didn't run far.
He realized that there might
be other people on the island
who were being forced to work
for Hydra. Sam decided to go
back and free them!
But he couldn't do it alone.
    Sam was trying to devise a
plan when he heard a noise
coming from the jungle.
He followed the sound and
found a falcon trapped in a net.
The bird was not hurt, but it
was unable to free itself. Sam
immediately felt a bond with
the falcon and released it.

Sam named the falcon Redwing. He prepared a message and told the bird to take it to anyone it could find.

Soon enough, Redwing returned with Captain America. When Sam told Cap of Red Skull's evil plans, the two decided to team up against Hydra.

But Sam would need to gear up for such a dangerous mission. Captain America called S.H.I.E.L.D. agent Phil Coulson, who delivered a special suit for Sam.

Falcon was born!

Along with Captain America and Redwing, he sneaked deep into the Isle of Exiles and freed the other prisoners.

Hydra was strong and powerful, but it was no match for such a mighty team. Even Red Skull's Cosmic Cube, which allowed Red Skull to bend the fabric of reality, could not save the Super Villain.

Together, the heroes defeated Cap's most dangerous enemy.

Sam knew it was time to return to New York. He could not run from his pain. He had to face it.

But Sam was not the scared boy he had once been. As Falcon, he could help make New York a safer place.

Falcon often partnered with Captain America. S.H.I.E.L.D. even made him a set of artificial wings that enabled him to fly.

Now Sam really was like a falcon.

Falcon proved himself time and again. Eventually, he was even asked to join the Avengers.

Earth's Mightiest Heroes gained a strong, loyal new member.

And Falcon found a family at last.

What Goes Up Must Come Down

One sunny morning in New York, Captain America decided to visit the Statue of Liberty. But time off doesn't last long when you're an Avenger, and he soon found himself called to action by the sound of screams.

"Look over there!" a tourist shouted, pointing across the water to Manhattan. Bicycles, cars and even people were flying into the air.

No bridge connected Liberty Island to the rest of Manhattan, and Cap didn't have time to wait for the next ferry. Using his communicator, he contacted his good friend and fellow Avenger, Falcon.

"Where to, Cap?" asked the winged hero, carrying Captain America across the water.

"Times Square, Falcon. I'm guessing the rest of the Avengers could probably use our help," Cap replied.

Captain America was right. The Avengers had their hands full, trying to rescue people from the strange change in gravity.

As tourists floated into the sky, Hawkeye shot arrows attached to nets and anchored people to the tops of lamp posts. Meanwhile, Hulk used his incredible strength to keep a bus filled with people from drifting into the air.

The airborne members of the Avengers did their part to save people, too.

"This is madness!" shouted Iron Man. "We can't rescue everyone."

"But that won't stop us from trying," replied Captain America, as he and Falcon arrived on the scene.

"What – or who – could be behind this?" asked Falcon.

"This seems most familiar," said Thor. "Perhaps it is the work of – "

Before Thor could finish, the face of the evil scientist Graviton appeared on one of Times Square's giant video screens.

"People of New York," the speakers blared, "I am Graviton. I do not wish to harm you. I seek only those costumed do-gooders who sent me to prison – the Avengers!"

Graviton had once been a brilliant scientist named Franklin Hall. An accident had given him control over gravity, which was why he had renamed himself Graviton. The Avengers had stopped him many times in the past. Now he had escaped from prison and was out for revenge.

"My demands are simple," Graviton continued. "Either the Avengers surrender themselves to me at noon today, or I will send the island of Manhattan and the Statue of Liberty into space!

"Noon," Graviton repeated. "And not a minute later."

With that, the screens went blank and gravity slowly returned to normal.

"We can't surrender!" exclaimed Hawkeye. "Graviton will just take us prisoner and go ahead with his plans anyway."

Iron Man agreed. "You're right. We can't trust Graviton, but he'll do tremendous harm if we don't give him what he wants."

The armoured Avenger paused. "I have a plan," he said at last. "*We* can't surrender, but *you* can."

Iron Man pointed at Captain America, Hawkeye and Black Widow!

At noon, Captain America, Hawkeye and Black Widow surrendered to Graviton, who used his powers to keep anyone else from coming near them.

"I never thought any of you would surrender," he gloated. Then added, "But embarrassing the Avengers was just the beginning....

"The real prize is the billion-dollar ransom I'll get for the island of Manhattan!" Graviton continued.

Suddenly, the Avengers felt the ground lurch beneath them, and the entire island of Manhattan floated into the air. To the south of the city, the Statue of Liberty rose off its base.

Cap threw his shield at the villain, knocking him unconscious.
As quickly as Manhattan had risen, it started to drop.
Luckily, Iron Man's plan was already working.

"Graviton was boasting so much he never saw your shield coming," Black Widow said. "Thor, Iron Man ... Graviton is down. You're up!"

High in the sky, the mighty Thor whirled his Asgardian hammer, Mjolnir, over his head, summoning storm clouds and creating an enormous rainstorm. "I shall not let you down," he told Black Widow. "Creating storms such as this is child's play. The wind and rain shall raise the sea level, slowing the isle of Manhattan's fall back to Earth – "

Suddenly, Iron Man interrupted on his communicator....

"As long as I do the hard part," Iron Man said, laughing. He flew at high speed in circles around the island, turning Thor's storm waters into a cushion on which he could gently lower the island back into place.

"We're all going to have a lot of repair work to do when this is over, Tony," Cap told his fellow Avenger.

"Speaking of repairs," added Iron Man, "Falcon, how's Lady Liberty?"

"Not to worry," Falcon replied. "She's holding up just fine, but you might want to hurry...."

Hulk had leaped to Liberty Island just in time to prevent the statue from smashing into the ground beneath it. Hulk groaned, straining under the weight, but not letting any harm come to the symbol of freedom. He shouted, "Other Avengers better come fix lady statue soon! Hulk love to smash … but Hulk hate lifting!"

Party Crashers

Billionaire inventor and scientist Tony Stark – better known as Iron Man – was hosting the annual Stark Expo. Scientists from around the world had gathered at his offices in New York City to unveil their latest inventions. This was their chance to show the scientific community what they had been working on.

Tony was leading the conference, but he was not alone. He had brought the Avengers with him. Tony knew that so much technology in one place was sure to attract attention, and he wanted to make sure that none of the scientists – or their inventions – fell into the wrong hands.

"With so many brilliant people working together," Tony Stark told his guests, "I know that we can make the world a better place. And so I would like to – "

Suddenly, Tony was interrupted by a booming voice at the other end of the hall – "These scientists and their inventions now belong to the Masters of Evil!"

The scientists gasped and turned around. Standing across the room were four of the most dangerous Super Villains in the world: Baron Zemo, Ultron, the Enchantress and Klaw. Each one was tough but when they worked together as the Masters of Evil, they were almost unstoppable.

Captain America sprang into action. The Super Hero launched himself at Baron Zemo, knocking the villain back with his unbreakable vibranium shield.

"Tony – suit up!" Cap yelled. Then, turning to the rest of his team, he cried, "Avengers, ASSEMBLE!"

Tony called his Iron Man armour to him. The pieces flew through the air and attached themselves to his body. Iron Man wasted no time. Firing his repulsors, he blasted a hole in the side of the wall for the scientists to escape through.

But before he could yell to them, a high-pitched sound blasted through the expo.

Klaw was using sound waves to stop the scientists from escaping. The high-pitched waves caused them to fall to the ground in pain.

Iron Man had heard enough. "Can you play any other tunes?" he asked. Iron Man fired a repulsor blast at Klaw that sent him crashing to the ground, and the horrible sound stopped.

On the other side of the expo, the Enchantress rose into the air. Looking around the room, she quickly focused her attention on a group of frightened scientists.

The Enchantress laughed. She knew that her magic was powerful, but with the help of the scientists' technology, she would be *unstoppable*!

Lifting her hand, the Enchantress fired an energy blast at the scientists. But her powers were blocked by Thor and his mighty hammer, Mjolnir! The energy bounced off the hammer and rebounded back at the Enchantress.

"Return thee to Midgard!" the Asgardian warrior yelled.

The Enchantress laughed again and created a protective shield around herself. The shield deflected the energy, leaving her unharmed. "I will leave Earth only with these scientists as my prisoners!" she hissed.

"Not today!" a voice yelled from behind. It was Black Widow.

The Enchantress's protective shield may have been powerful against magic, but it could not stop pure physical force. Black Widow delivered a powerful blow to the unsuspecting villainess, knocking her out cold.

With the villainess out of the way, Black Widow turned to see where else she could be of help.

Across the room, the scientists ran for the exit. But they did not get far. Ultron and his terrible robots were blocking the way.

Black Widow tried to get to the scientists, but there were too many robots.

"Hawkeye!" she called.

Hawkeye lifted a special electric arrow from his quiver and fired it at one of the robots, causing it to short out.

"Get to the other exit," he yelled to the scientists.

The scientists fled to the other side of the room ... all but one.

Dr Bruce Banner stood beside Hawkeye, taking in the situation around him.

"You know," Hawkeye called over his shoulder as he drew and fired another arrow, "we could really use the big guy's help right now."

Bruce nodded. It was a good thing these robots were making him angry.

Focusing his energy, Bruce let his rage flow freely. Suddenly, his hands and feet began to grow bigger. His shoulders grew wider and his shirt tore off his back.

Bruce let out an angry roar. But he wasn't Bruce anymore. He was the incredible Hulk!

"Hulk smash!" Hulk roared. With a mighty swing of his arm, he knocked over three of Ultron's robots.

Ultron was not going down without a fight. Raising his arms, he commanded his robotic army to attack Hulk.

The robots charged and blasted Hulk. It looked like the green Goliath was outmatched – until Iron Man, Falcon and Thor joined the fight.

"You're the perfect example of technology gone bad," Iron Man yelled to Ultron as he fired one repulsor blast after another.

"On the contrary, I am the perfect example of technology!" the villain replied. And as his robotic minions attacked the Avengers, Ultron snuck off to join the other Masters of Evil.

Baron Zemo, Ultron, Klaw and the Enchantress regrouped in the centre of the expo. "The Avengers are formidable adversaries," Baron Zemo began. "If they will not let us leave with the scientists, then we will destroy the entire expo. Prepare for our escape – I will set the explosives!"

"Not so fast!" a voice yelled behind them. The villains turned. Much to their surprise, they saw the scientists – and their technology – blocking their escape.

"You're not going anywhere," a familiar voice called out from the opposite side of the room. It was Captain America and the Avengers. The Super Heroes and the scientists had the Super Villains surrounded. There was nowhere left for them to go and nothing left for them to do but surrender!

After S.H.I.E.L.D. took away the Masters of Evil, the Stark Expo restarted over and Iron Man addressed the crowd. "Our future depends on science and technology. And with all of us working together – like we just did today – I know that we can make the world a better place. And I know that the Avengers – and all of you – will always be there to protect it!"

Battle For Earth

It was a quiet night. The Avengers were enjoying a well-deserved rest when an explosion rocked the Natural History Museum.
The Avengers arrived at the scene to see Thanos – one of the most dangerous villains in the universe.

Thanos was looking for an ancient artefact – the magical Sword of Histria.

The Super Villain fired a blast of energy at Captain America using his Infinity Gauntlet, a magic glove that drew its energy from six powerful gems.

Captain America quickly raised his indestructible shield. But Thanos was very powerful. The force of his blast threw Captain America backwards into his fellow Avenger, Falcon.

"You humans are no match for me," the villain bellowed as he moved deeper into the museum. "Once I have the Sword of Histria, I will slice your beloved planet Earth in two!"

Hawkeye moved into position to stop the Super Villain, but Thanos was faster than the hero had imagined. Before Hawkeye could even lift his bow, Thanos spun around and blasted the archer off his feet!

Turning back around, Thanos smashed the glass case that protected the Sword of Histria.

Thanos laughed as he took hold of the magical artefact.

"The Sword is mine!" he roared triumphantly. "My plan is almost complete. No one will be able to stop me now."

Captain America and Black Widow charged towards Thanos, but they were too late.

With an evil laugh, the Super Villain teleported away with the Sword, leaving Cap and Black Widow to look after an injured Hawkeye and Falcon.

High above the ground, hidden among the clouds, hovered the massive S.H.I.E.L.D. Helicarrier, headquarters of the world's best super spies.

On board, the Avengers met with Nick Fury, the director of S.H.I.E.L.D.

"We know why Thanos stole the Sword of Histria and what his ultimate plan is," Captain America told the group. "What we don't know is where he's going."

"According to intel on the Sword, it's powerless unless it's returned to the place it was created," Iron Man said.

Nick Fury shook his head. "That could be anywhere."

Just then, Special Agent Ruby, who specialized in ancient artifacts, joined the group.

"Maybe I can help," Agent Ruby said. "The Sword was being held for safekeeping at the Natural History Museum, but my sources say it was created at Castle Aarole in the Carpathian Mountains."

Agent Ruby pulled up an image of the castle.

Nick Fury looked at the image, then turned to the group. "Looks like you're going to Romania."

The Avengers wasted no time. They boarded the Quinjet and raced to Romania.

The heroes soon arrived at Castle Aarole. But Thanos had beaten them there. As the Avengers rushed toward him, the Sword of Histria began to glow with ancient energy. It was very close to the place it had been forged.

The Avengers had to stop Thanos, and fast. They were the planet's last hope. They sprang into action, but Thanos wasn't going down without a fight.

Thor and Hulk pressed the attack. While Thor threw his enchanted hammer, Mjolnir, at Thanos, Hulk smashed his fists into the ground. Shock waves radiated out, shaking the earth. But Thanos had drawn extra energy from the Sword of Histria. He was now more powerful than ever and he easily deflected Thor's hammer, as well as withstanding Hulk's shock waves.

As the Sword pulsed with magical energy, Thanos stepped over the crumbled outer castle wall. Just a few more feet and the Sword would be at full power.

Iron Man raced in to stop Thanos, but the Super Villain used the power of the Sword to short-circuit Iron Man's armour. As Thanos continued forwards, he fired an energy blast at Hulk. Thanos knew the blast would only temporarily blind Hulk, but it would give him the time he needed.

With Hulk out of the way, Thanos swept past the rest of the Avengers and into the ancient castle.

Behind him, Black Widow fired electrostatic bolts from her bracelets. But she was too late! The energy had no effect on the Super Villain. Thanos had reached his destination – the very spot where the Sword of Histria had been created so many centuries earlier.

As Thanos raised the sword triumphantly in the air, a swirl of colourful lights appeared in the sky above him, temporarily blinding the Avengers. The blaze of energy engulfed Thanos and the mystical Sword.

The ground shook and cracked beneath the Avengers' feet. The air, charged with magical power, crackled around them. Had Thanos won?

The Avengers needed another plan....

Iron Man's armour was useless, but Tony Stark's genius-level mind was not. He had a plan. They couldn't defeat Thanos as long as he had the Sword. But they *could* destroy the Sword itself.

Thor used Mjolnir to bring down the lightning and empower Captain America's shield with Asgardian energy.

Iron Man turned to Hulk. "We need your strength," he said.

At Iron Man's direction, Hulk hurled Cap's energized shield at the Sword of Histria.

Thanos, focused on the sword, did not realize that he was under attack. He was preparing to slice the earth in two when suddenly he saw a red, white and blue blur zooming towards him. There was no time for him to act.

Captain America's shield, powered by Thor's Asgardian energy and the superhuman strength of the incredible Hulk, struck the Sword of Histria. Thanos managed to jump back, but he could not save the weapon. The magical artefact shattered into a thousand pieces.

The Sword's ancient energies were released, causing an enormous explosion that knocked Thanos back. Pieces of the sword fell to the ground around him.

Thanos knew he was defeated. His stolen sword was broken and his plans for the destruction of Earth were at an end.

The triumphant Avengers surrounded Thanos, but the Super Villain would not allow himself to be captured. As they closed in on him, Thanos teleported away.

The Avengers knew Thanos would return one day to finish what he'd started, and when he did, Earth's Mightiest Heroes would be there to stop him!

Kang – Conqueror of S.H.I.E.L.D.

Kang was bored. He was a conquerer, but the 31st century had nothing left to conquer. He had conquered Earth. He had conquered the moon. He had even conquered the common cold!

Kang sighed. "I look upon my kingdom and I weep, for I have no more worlds to conquer. No more rulers to overthrow or lands to –"

Suddenly, Kang grew quiet. He had just come up with the most delightfully sinister idea he'd ever had – he could travel back in time and conquer the world all over again!

Kang laughed triumphantly.

"Once again, Kang will conquer all!" the Super Villain yelled.

Meanwhile, in the 21st century, S.H.I.E.L.D. agent Maria Hill was excited. The Avengers had been fighting more villains than usual lately. That meant Maria and her crew had been too busy to do all the odd jobs needed to keep her department running smoothly. Now, with the Avengers away on a longer mission, she finally had time to do some much-needed maintenance on the S.H.I.E.L.D. Helicarrier.

"Seize the day, gentlemen," Maria shouted. "We don't get many quiet moments around here. Let's use this time to clear the backlog of reports we have to write and make sure the engines are in tip-top shape."

Maria looked around and shuddered. The Helicarrier was filthy. She couldn't let it stay that way.

"Let's scrub these floors and clean our desks, equipment and boots before the Avengers return," she said.

The crew jumped into action, preparing to follow each of Maria's orders.

Across the bridge, Director Nick Fury monitored the Avengers. They were responding to a bizarre threat in South America – several dinosaurs had appeared out of thin air and begun eating everything in sight!

Nick watched as Hulk threw a punch at a T. rex. Iron Man flew around the vicious creature, trying to distract it. The T. rex snapped its jaws, narrowly missing Captain America.

Nick sat back, enjoying the show. The dinosaurs didn't stand a chance against Earth's Mightiest Heroes.

"Never a dull moment with them," Fury said as Thor flew into view.

"You can say that again!" Maria said. "Which is why we need to get things done as quickly as possible. Who *knows* when the next disaster is going to strike!"

Agent Hill smiled as the crew tightened bolts on machines, emptied desk drawers and even did the dishes.

"I love it when a plan comes together," she exclaimed.

"I wouldn't call this a victory just yet," Fury remarked from a weather console. "Instruments show that the Helicarrier is headed into some kind of storm front like nothing we've ever seen before."

Just then, purple and green lightning flashed through the windows.
"What kind of lightning bolts are those?" Maria asked.
"The kind that follow the thunderclaps of history's mightiest time storm," a voice boomed. It was Kang.
"The future belongs to Kang," the conqueror explained, appearing on the bridge. "And now, so shall the past!"

Turning, Kang fired a blast at a nearby crew member. To Maria's amazement, Kang's blasts didn't destroy the people and objects they hit – they *aged* them. Steel consoles rusted, and glass warped and cracked.

"With the Avengers away, no one can stop me from aging S.H.I.E.L.D. to dust," the villain explained. "And then the past will belong to Kang the Conqueror, just like the future."

"The dinosaurs in South America – you brought them here to keep the Avengers busy?" Nick Fury asked.

"Of course," Kang said, cackling. "All of time – past, present and future – is at my disposal."

Fury threw a switch and a force field lowered over Kang.

"Didn't see *that* coming, did you?" Fury laughed.

"You fools," Kang cried.
"Do you really believe your puny tricks can stop me? I am a time traveller. I will call on a future self to free me."

At that moment, another Kang appeared. Hitting a button, he freed the trapped Kang.

Nick Fury turned to Maria Hill. "This is starting to give me a headache," he said.

"No kidding," a heroic voice shouted from above.

Both Kangs spun around to see the mighty Avengers.

The Avengers had tamed the dinosaurs. Now, the powerful beasts fought *with* them.

Hulk's T. rex gave a rumbling roar as the heroes surrounded the time-travelling villains.

"What doth thine reptilian beast say?" Thor asked Hulk.

Hulk smiled. "T. rex say 'SMASH!'"

"You heard him!" Iron Man called.

With that, the Avengers – and their dinosaurs – charged towards the Kangs.

The Kangs had seen enough of history to realize they were hopelessly outmatched by the collective power of Earth's Mightiest Heroes.

"Until next time, heroes." Kang called out as he and his older self leaped forwards into the future.

As the dust settled and things returned to normal, Iron Man turned to Captain America. "This place is a wreck," he said.

"Iron Man's right, Agent Hill," Cap began. "When is S.H.I.E.L.D. going to start cleaning up around here?"

Maria Hill sighed as Nick Fury gave her a wink with his good eye.

"No time like the present," he said.

Call For Backup

Billionaire inventor Tony Stark loved new technology. His company, Stark Industries, had been hard at work on a new spaceship that could safely take groups of tourists to the moon. Finally, it was ready for its first flight.

Putting on his Iron Man armour, Tony flew alongside the ship as it blasted off.

A short time later, Iron Man greeted the ship's passengers at the new Stark Industries Moon Base. Iron Man had invited very important people, including leaders in government and business from all around the world, to be part of the first group to visit the base.

Suddenly, the tourists' fun was interrupted by a huge crash.

"Don't worry," Iron Man assured the group. "It's probably nothing dangerous. I'll go check it out."

But secretly, Iron Man was worried. *What could have caused that crash?* he wondered as he rocketed towards the crash site.

Iron Man called his teammates, the Avengers, to help.

"We're in the middle of a battle with Hydra," said Captain America over the communicator. "We'll get there as soon as we can, but it could take some time."

For now, Iron Man was on his own!

Iron Man was right to be worried. Emerging from the crash site was Thanos, an evil ruler from deep space who wanted nothing more than to take over Earth.

And Thanos wasn't alone. He had brought along his army of Outriders – a race of alien warriors, each with four strong arms, long claws and razor-sharp teeth.

Iron Man was in serious trouble. With the Avengers occupied, he called the only other group that might be able to help.

Deep in space, on the bridge of their mighty starship, the Guardians of the Galaxy received Iron Man's distress call.

"Tony Stark's in trouble," reported Star-Lord, the brave leader of the Guardians.

"Let's go," said Drax, a fierce alien soldier.

"How can we get there in time?" asked the green-skinned Gamora. "We're halfway across the galaxy!"

"I am Groot," remarked the plant creature, Groot.

"Good point, Groot," said Rocket Raccoon, a small but skilled mercenary. Groot only ever said "I am Groot," but Rocket always knew what he meant. "Groot thinks we should ask the Nova Corps for a boost."

Star-Lord radioed the Nova Corps, a group of interstellar peacekeepers. "We need an emergency teleport to Earth's moon," he said.

Happy to help, the Novas quickly initiated a teleportation beam that sent the Guardians through space.

As soon as the Guardians arrived, they jumped into battle.

"What took you so long?" complained Iron Man, who had been forced to the ground by the Outriders.

"We come all the way from the other side of the galaxy, and this is the thanks we get?" asked Rocket.

"I am Groot," added Groot.

"Time for battle!" yelled Gamora, smashing the Outriders.

"Guardians, don't hold back on these guys," ordered Star-Lord.
Forced to fight the Guardians, the Outriders backed off Iron Man.
The armoured Avenger was able to pick himself up and defend
himself against his attackers.
"You sure know how to get into trouble, Stark," joked Rocket.

While the Guardians and Iron Man were fighting the Outriders, Thanos headed towards the moon base.

That's when Iron Man understood Thanos's plan. "He must be trying to capture everyone at the base," Iron Man said. "So many of Earth's important leaders are there. Thanos could grab them all at once."

Without its greatest leaders, the planet would be weaker. Thanos could invade and proclaim himself ruler.

But Thanos didn't get far. At that moment, the mighty Avengers arrived in their Quinjet.

"Avengers, assemble!" shouted Captain America, directing the team in combat.

"That's right. If you want a shot at Earth, you'll have to go through us first," Hawkeye announced.

"Hulk smash!" yelled the battle-ready Hulk, racing towards Thanos.

The Avengers combined their powers and abilities in an attempt to stop Thanos.

"Have at thee, villain!" Thor shouted, hurling his mighty hammer.

"That goes for all of us," Falcon agreed as he swooped in.

"We will stop you, Thanos," promised Black Widow.

But despite the team's best efforts, Thanos was still gaining ground.

Iron Man scanned Thanos and discovered something new.
"That device at his belt – he's never had that before," he said.
"Could that machine be what helped Thanos travel here?"

Thanos had arrived on the moon in a big crash. But Iron Man
didn't see a ship anywhere, and Thanos was unharmed. He must
have used some kind of new technology.

Quickly, Iron Man formed a plan. He needed Groot. The little plant creature held some big secrets.

"I'm going to need your special talents here, buddy," Iron Man said to Groot.

"I am Groot," replied Groot.

"You bet you are!" agreed Iron Man.

Iron Man flew Groot over Thanos and dropped him right into the middle of the fight.

"Bombs away!" the armoured Avenger shouted.

As he fell, Groot transformed from a little plant into a giant plant.

"What is this?" asked the surprised Thanos, as Groot seemed to appear out of nowhere.

"I am Groot!" Groot yelled, delivering blow after crushing blow to Thanos.

Thanos was so distracted by Groot's sudden attack that he didn't notice Iron Man swoop in and steal the device from his belt.

Studying the device, Iron Man figured out how to reverse its effects. He pressed a button and a sphere of energy formed around Thanos and the Outriders.

With another push of a button, Iron Man sent the villains shooting away from the surface of the moon.

"Nooooo!" Thanos screamed as he flew away.

"Where are you sending them, Tony?" asked Captain America.

"Back to where they came from," responded Iron Man. "Without this device, we won't see them back here anytime soon."

Back on the moon base, Earth's leaders and their families were happy to be safe from Thanos and eager to meet their heroes. Thanks to the Avengers and their friends, the Guardians of the Galaxy, the trip to the moon was a great success!

An Unexpected Hero

Agent Phil Coulson was in his office aboard S.H.I.E.L.D.'s top-secret plane when a call came in from his boss, Nick Fury.

"I'm sending you to Egypt, Coulson," Fury said. "There are strange signals coming from some long-abandoned ruins and I need you to check it out."

Coulson nodded. "I'll have the plane change course at once," he replied.

Coulson arrived at the ruins and turned on the plane's scanners. Something was *definitely* wrong. The energy readings were off the charts.

Coulson carefully approached the ruins. Hidden behind a pile of bricks was a strange door.

Coulson walked through the door and looked around.
He expected to see a dusty tomb or a library of old scrolls.
Instead, he found a high-tech lab.

Agent Coulson studied the unusual equipment. "These systems
are so advanced!" he exclaimed. "I've never seen anything like them."

"That's because *I* invented them," a voice said. It was Ultron.

"Welcome, Agent Coulson," Ultron said with a laugh. "I was hoping you would join me."

Agent Coulson backed up, but he was trapped. The robotic Super Villain was blocking the only exit.

"I don't know what you're planning, Ultron," Coulson began, "but –"

Suddenly, Coulson stopped talking. Ultron had thrown a disk at him that made him freeze in place.

In New York, the Avengers were finishing a battle against A.I.M., a group of evil scientists bent on ruling the world.

"Come on, guys. A doom ray?" taunted Iron Man. "How unimaginative. I thought you A.I.M. guys would do better than that!"

Just then, a large figure appeared in the sky above the Avengers.

"Isn't that your Hulkbuster armour?" Falcon asked Iron Man. Iron Man had designed a special armoured suit that was as tough as Hulk himself.

"Ha," sneered Hulk. "Puny armour. Hulk is strongest one there is."

"We know that, big guy," Iron Man assured Hulk. "But that *is* one of my suits. What's it doing here?"

Before anyone could answer, the Hulkbuster armour suddenly attacked.

"Look out!" Captain America cried, raising his shield.

The Hulkbuster landed, and Thor ripped off its helmet. Inside was a gagged Agent Coulson.

Iron Man removed the gag. "What are you doing in my suit?" he asked the agent.

"Ultron froze me with some strange disk and then shoved me inside," Coulson explained. "I've been trapped in here for hours."

"Don't worry, Coulson, we'll get you out of there," Iron Man
assured the agent. "I just need to get you back to my armoury. Hulk?"
Hulk grunted and picked up the suit. With Coulson over his
shoulder, he followed the other Avengers to Iron Man's armoury.
Inside were all the suits Iron Man had created over the years.

Iron Man plugged Coulson and the Hulkbuster armour into his computer. Almost immediately, a loud alarm started to sound.

"The armour uploaded some kind of computer virus into the armoury's systems," Iron Man cried.

"That's right, Stark," a voice announced. It was Ultron! He had followed Coulson back to New York and all the way to Iron Man's armoury.

"You fools are so predictable," Ultron said. "I knew you would bring your agent here to free him."

Iron Man walked to a control panel and pushed a button. Nothing happened.

Ultron laughed. "My virus is in your computer system," he said. "Your armoury belongs to me."

Ultron raised his arms and Iron Man's collection of spare suits rose into the air.

"And now, Avengers, let's see how you do against not one, but an *army* of Iron Men," screamed Ultron.

The empty suits surrounded the heroes. Then, at Ultron's command, they attacked.

From inside the Hulkbuster, Agent Coulson watched the Avengers battle the empty suits.

I wish I could be out there, fighting with them, he thought.

"These mere empty shells cannot defeat us," proclaimed Thor as he pounded one of the heavier suits with his hammer.

"Especially not when we work together," agreed Captain America. "Avengers, assemble!"

Working together, the Avengers broke apart one suit after another.
"You see, Ultron," said Iron Man, "even when we're outnumbered,
the Avengers will always defeat evil."

But Ultron just laughed. "Once again, you did just as I had hoped.
Thank you for saving me the trouble of breaking these suits apart myself."

Ultron raised his arms again, and the pieces of armour that were scattered throughout the room flew towards him. One by one, the pieces attached to his metal body – making him bigger, stronger and more powerful than ever!

"Behold *Mega-Ultron*," shouted Ultron, "the greatest robot of all time."

The Avengers battled bravely against the new, improved Ultron – but he was too strong. "I can't believe it!" cried Hawkeye. "Even with all of us fighting him, he's still winning."

Behind them, unnoticed, Iron Man's computer continued to work. Suddenly, there was a faint *click* and the Hulkbuster armour popped open.

Agent Coulson reached into the armour and picked up the disk Ultron had used to freeze him. "Maybe I can use Ultron's own plan against him," he said.

With Ultron distracted, Coulson climbed the armour racks to a spot above the giant robot. Then, taking a deep breath, he leaped towards Ultron.

Coulson reached out with the disk and –

BAM! The disk attached to Ultron, who instantly froze in place!

"Smart thinking, son of Coul," Thor said. "You tricked Ultron. Very Loki of you."

"I'm glad I was able to help," said Coulson, pleased.

"If you want to help, come up here and get all these pieces off Ultron." shouted Iron Man. "I hope you're good at jigsaw puzzles, because we need to fix *all* of my suits."

As he helped put together the Iron Man suits, Coulson smiled. He was proud to fight beside the Avengers and call them friends.

The End